MICE IN SOPHIE'S MATTRESS

~An allegory of tenacity, adaptability and acceptance~

JERRY RAAF

Mill Lake Books

Mill Lake Books
Abbotsford, BC
Canada
https://jamescoggins.wordpress.com/mill-lake-books/

Cover design by Dean Tjepkema

ISBN: 978-0-9951983-6-4

A GIFT TO

____

FROM

____

DATE

____

This book is dedicated to a special friend.
His future was challenged at six months old
when his parents and brother were killed in
an auto accident.
Years later, his lovely and talented wife
passed away from cancer.
Slings and arrows of outrageous misfortune
have pummelled him, made holes in his
heart and gnawed at his integrity.
Disappointment has pursued him.
People have taken advantage of him.
Yet he is STRONG, and I envy his tenacity,
grit and optimism.
He is a model of a man.
I salute you, Sir.

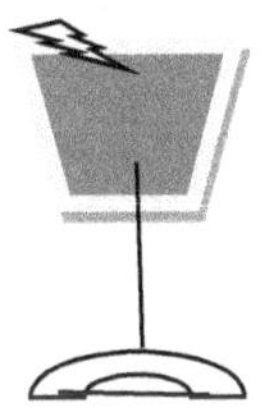

~ KURP ~

TABLE of CONTENTS

Chapter 1

A PLEASANT PLACE TO SEE

From a distance the Brunzhoffa farmyard, with a large white two-story farmhouse and roof dormers, appeared as peaceful as a Norman Rockwell painting. The picket fences were straight and newly painted, hundreds of various colored flowers swayed everywhere in the gentle summer breezes, the flock of sheep in the meadow near the shallow slough were fat and appeared domesticated, cows stood quietly in the shade of the two-story red barn, and fat feathered fowl scratched and pecked at the earth as they searched for bugs and seeds near the garden and granaries. Several noisy white ducks waddled near a small patch of quack grass next to the sidewalk that led to the outhouse, and multi-colored laundry continuously danced on the wash line, which was fastened at one end to the back porch of the farmhouse and was attached at the other end to a large deciduous tree near the outhouse.

Near the entrance of the barn, a plump Clydesdale mare and her colt swished their tails at flies and insects. Three tilting scarecrows attempted to guard the lush garden nearby but sadly provided only comfortable perches for dozens of black-feathered obnoxious corn thieves. Even the bales of hay in the meadow lay in straight lines, while on the porch of the farmhouse a scruffy long-haired Old English Sheepdog named Oatmeal slept facing the public roadway that passed this idyllic place. On the porch handrail lay an oversized well-fed orange cat named Marmalade who spent most of the day licking his fur, and on the bottom steps of the porch was a dark brown fat cat named Fudge. It was a picture too perfect for reality.

Near the irregularly shaped slough, some distance from the back of the barn, were dozens of tall cattails and water reeds. Here Red-Winged Blackbirds chirped and sang their hypnotic songs while Meadow Larks flapped their wings and stretched their necks to warble their praise to their Creator. Frogs croaked in what seemed to be a never ending contest to declare that they were the kings of the pond. Dragonflies hovered over the surface of the rippling water as if they were admiring their own reflection.

This coveted farmyard was owned and carefully manicured by Herb and Sophie Brunzhoffa, a persnickety aging couple whose reputation and self-worth hinged upon neatness and public image.

Neighbors and fellow worshippers at St. Matthew's Anglican Church and St. John's Roman Catholic Church respected these citizens for their kindness and their giving hearts. Sophie always knitted colorful shawls for the needy and baked many pies for community bazaars, while Herb worked tirelessly in his shop during the long winter months to make wooden toys for less fortunate children in Thistle, a small country town with three tilting grain elevators that sadly needed repair and paint.

Every morning Herb left the house wearing clean bib overalls, a colorful plaid shirt and his favorite straw hat. Even his work boots were polished, and the gloves that hung out of his rear pocket were a matched pair. He milked three cows — Bessy, Bossy and Flossy — fed dozens of various colored chickens and four noisy ducks, gave ground oats and garden scraps to six noisy hogs and then returned to the kitchen for his predicable breakfast of bacon and eggs served with three buttermilk flapjacks and strong black coffee. As far as Herb was concerned, everything was great except for the back pain he experienced every morning which usually lasted until noon.

Sophie insisted that it was the forty-seven-year-old bed that caused the predictable pain, and she had, over the years, become tired of preaching the same message to Herb. She was convinced he did not hear what she was saying or he was simply ignoring her suggestion because replacing the mattress would cost too much money. Neighbors considered Herb to be thrifty and careful with his coins, but Sophie secretly considered him to be just plain cheap.

"That old bed sags like a hundred-year-old hammock well past its prime," she muttered as she buttered his rye toast. "I've told you many times that we need a new mattress, like the ones advertised at Cuthbert's Furniture Store."

Sophie's words were always presented in kindness with nary a hint of confrontation.

Their sedentary lives, however, changed the day Herb dropped Sophie off at Marten's Pharmacy in Thistle, a rural town in western Canada. Change was imminent the moment Sophie stepped through the front doors of the pharmacy, where she began to gather several personal items for purchase, such as: Evening Breeze perfume, Smooth and Gentle Hand Lotion, a tube of Colgate toothpaste and two pairs of knitted nylon stockings, the kind usually worn by short and slightly overweight grannies who wear their hair in a bun.

"That will be five dollars and ninety-seven cents," said Mrs. Galway as Sophie pulled out her change purse with the snap at the top. Mrs. Galway knew the full amount would be paid to the penny with coins from within that hand-knitted coin purse.

"Sophie, why bother with all that change every time you buy something? Why not sign up for one of those fancy new credit cards that everyone is using? It's so easy. All you do is hand us your credit card and we put it into this here machine," she said as she pointed at it. "You just swipe it and you walk out of here with whatever you have purchased, a-n-d — " she dragged out the word for emphasis before continuing her sentence — "at the end of the month Visa mails you the bill . . . and then you pay what you owe at the bank." Her smile and tone of voice enticed trust.

"Oh, Herb wouldn't be happy with that, I'm sure," she said as she smiled and returned the coin purse into her larger purse. "He doesn't trust banks and insists that only cash is for sure."

"Sophie, this is the seventies. Banks won't cheat you, and credit cards are the in-thing. Every lady in this town has one, and they even use it to buy groceries. I have two of them." She paused momentarily as she reached for an application form and then searched for a pen next to the cash register. "Here, I'll help you fill it out, and when the card arrives in your mailbox, you can surprise Herb."

"Do you really think so? What does it cost?" There was a note of suspicious caution in her voice.

"Nothing, absolutely nothing, just your signature. So sit down and I'll help you fill out the application form. It's easy," insisted Mrs. Galway. She tilted her head to one side as a smile transformed her elderly face into that of a rather youthful looking trusted friend.

"Well, if it's that easy . . . OK," responded Sophie as she adjusted her wire-rimmed bifocals and reached for the ballpoint pen that Mrs. Galway held in her hand.

"Here's a pen," Mrs. Galway said. "Now print your name, NO, not your last name but your first name . . . S.o.p.h.i.e. . . . and now print your last name, B.r.u.n.z.h.o.f.f.a. — good and . . . on this line print your mailing address. Finish the form while I serve Maris Boese who just came into the store with her unruly nephew . . . then . . . I'll be right back."

When Mrs. Galway returned, she glanced through the application form to ensure it was filled out correctly. "Oh, Sophie," she said, "You didn't put in how much money your husband earned last year."

"But I don't know, so what should I put down cause we only have a small farm and sell eggs and milk for grocery money and . . . occasionally Herb sells hay to the horse farm near Weyburn and . . . and we sold several hogs at a farm auction two weeks ago."

"Banks don't look at those numbers, I'm sure, so I'll write in, ah . . . let me see, how about $2,000 . . . so you sign it and seal the envelope. I'll mail it for you, and soon you'll have your own credit card. Your first purchase will be so much fun. Trust me."

Sophie tried desperately to hide her excitement, but her smile was anchored deep inside, somewhere beyond mischievous and playfully naughtiness. It contained no malice or spiteful intent, only impish glee.

Sophie decided to keep her secret about the credit card application from Herb. She rolled up the window as Herb drove their noisy and faded 1956 Ford pickup truck along the rough and dusty country road. Mile after mile, she massaged her hands with the hand cream she had purchased at Marten's Pharmacy and wondered how she would break the news to Herb about the Visa card, and then she dreamed of what her first purchase would be.

On the way home, Herb and Sophie stopped at Leo and Edna's house for supper. Sophie was so excited to tell Edna, her sister-in-law, about her application for a modern day credit card. She insisted several times that Edna keep her secret from Leo and Herb.

Following supper, the men sat on the porch and shared a pint of bubbly ale and roll-your-own cigarettes. They speculated about fuel prices and costs to grow grain next year.

Meanwhile Sophie told Edna that her first purchase would be a new mattress and box spring. They spent the better part of two hours looking through the Cuthbert's Furniture sales page, found in the local weekly newspaper.

It was well after nine p.m. when Herb and Sophie started for home. They drove in silence, and when Herb stopped the truck in front of their farmhouse, the headlights of their truck shone on Oatmeal, the shaggy

Sheepdog, who was waiting on the front porch. When Herb shut off the headlights, he stepped from the truck and look up at the sky. He and Sophie remained motionless as they stared at the millions of stars that seemed to hang over their farm in the night sky. The harvest moon seemed so yellow and so round against the satin ebony sky. Off in the distance several coyotes called to each other just as Sophie started up the front steps of the porch.

Somewhere near the barnyard, one of the cows began lowing because she was expecting to have been milked several hours earlier. Sophie flipped the switch to turn on the yard light so Herb and Oatmeal could make their way to the barn. Sometime later, Herb returned to the house with both pails full of milk, and shortly after that he started the cream separator.

By midnight, Herb was curled up in bed as Sophie sat on the edge of the bed. Suddenly she gave a loud shriek that caused Herb to sit up. The bed bounced several times as Sophie reached for the flashlight on the night table.

"WHAT'S THE MATTER?" yelled Herb.

"Something moved across my hand and I . . . I think it was a mouse."

"Well, is it still there?"

"No . . ." she whispered.

"Well, don't worry about one mouse in an old house this size. Where are those over-fed cats when you need them?" he muttered as he turned to face the window and pulled the faded blanket over his shoulder.

"I've set a dozen traps, but I never catch any mice, and now before I go to sleep, one finds me," she giggled as she rubbed her hand and arm.

"Say your prayers, and God will keep them away from you. Good night, Dear" mumbled Herb as he closed his eyes.

"Good night, Deary," Sophie whispered as she slumped into the sagging mattress that caused her to roll into Herb. When she had stopped bouncing and rolling, she pulled the blankets up to her chin and sighed loudly as she shut her eyes.

"Herb . . ."

"What now? Another mouse?"

"I've been so busy that I forgot to remind you that the Community Fair is scheduled in two days. I assume we're going?"

"Ah yahhh," Herb responded as he started to yawn. When he finished his yawn, his next breath began his primitive nocturnal breathing with its predictable cadence.

Outside, coyotes continued to call in the moonlight, and soon Oatmeal responded with several loud barks to warn them that he was still on guard. His deep-chested bark must have been sufficient warning because the choir of coyotes became silent.

Chapter 2

SOPHIE'S HOUSE GUESTS

Giuseppe (Ju-sep-ee) and his best friends Patrizio (Pat-rees-seo) and Angelo were inseparable mice that lived in Sophie and Herb's house. They were much more than friends and considered themselves to be blood brothers. Most of the resident rodents who lived in the old two-story farmhouse believed that they were triplets; however, only their mothers knew the truth.

Giuseppe was a popular resident because of his ability to race from the basement to the second floor of the old farmhouse. No one could match his speed, agility and technique as he sped through heating ducts, over electrical wires, along dusty baseboards, under tattered rugs, along the armrests of faded couches and up and over tattered curtains. His record times were seldom challenged.

Patrizio was envied for his strong tenor voice. He sang classical opera such as "Sole a Mia," "O Mio Babbino Caro," "Ava Maria" and "Voi Che Sapete." Everyone who listened to him stood in mesmerized silence, their breathing synchronized to each word and phrase. His demeanor and delivery made him a perfect crooner, and his smile charmed every female from three to thirteen. They swooned at his long curly hair that swayed when he sang.

Angelo had great skills as a dancer. The daily races throughout the Brunzhoffa residence provided him with confident footwork and balance, but when music from Sophie's transistor radio or records was being played, his legs seemed to come alive.

Patrizio and Angelo memorized each song and phrase from the classical music which Sophie, the lady of the house, played on a small transistor radio tuned into the CBC radio station based in the city of Regina. Also, Sophie constantly played her collection of classical records during the day and late evening. She worshipped the artistry of Maria Callas and Luciano Pavarotti.

Every Thursday evening, Patrizio and Angelo would present their talents in the basement of the old farmhouse as fans watched nearby. Every cardboard box became an observation perch, the stairs were packed with eager fans, and every outside windowsill on the ground floor of the house was packed with various sized mice, some of whom resided in the red barn next to the granaries. Occasionally large field mice attended and eagerly elbowed their way to the windows to enjoy the music.

There never was a day when the three special friends were not together, sharing food and playing rowdy rodent games from dawn 'til dusk. Their world was a haven where want was unknown. Their youthful days were filled with games, racing and other good-time activities. Surrounded with many friends and family members, they witnessed few conflicts and enjoyed plenteous food, comfortable beds and constant warmth, so they had little to hope for or wish for. If asked what else they needed or desired, they would have responded, 'To live carefree forever.'

Youthful and strong, able to run, play and sing at will, they knew only pleasure, popularity and comfort. Their world existed on two floors and the basement of an old white two-story farmhouse, which was filled with tasty foods and abundant hero worship.

The only potential enemies any of them had were two well-fed, lazy housecats: Marmalade, a bright almost fluorescent orange feline, and Fudge, a dark brown almost black colored fat cat. Both were greatly sated from what Sophie, the lady of the house, placed in their saucers next to the wood and coal kitchen stove. These tubby tabbies spent all of their time licking their fur and lying in the warm sunshine that bathed the front porch and the kitchen window sills

Three separate and peaceful groups of rodents coexisted in the white farmhouse where Giuseppe, Angelo and Patrizio spent their days carrying out their usual forays and other robust rodent activities. Giuseppe and his family lived on the top floor of the old house, Angelo's family lived on the main floor, and Patrizio and his family members lived in the basement. The adult mice were careful to share all foods, yet they tried to live independent lives.

They seldom discussed their family history and only remembered shards of ancient history told to them by old grey-whiskered rotund relatives at night under the warm kitchen stove. The stories of former relatives living in a country in a faraway land meant little to them when they tried to imagine what life was like back then.

They could not comprehend the difficulties of yesteryear when pantries were empty. Now, tasty pastas, spicy meats, cheeses and tomato flavoured sauces were constantly available in larders bulging with foods prepared and stored by Sophie.

Often the aged rodents would warn the younger generations of hard times to come, when families could be separated, food might be scarce, and major injuries and death would likely be commonplace.

"These good times will not always be here for us," was the common warning given to the youthful generation by grey-whiskered, crippled and feeble family members. "Beware — because good times will not last forever, and when bad times come, and they will come . . . then you'll remember our words."

It was a message unheeded.

****

The farmhouse was a lively place with one hundred and eighty-seven mice living in the basement and one hundred and twenty-four living on the main floor in the folds of the old sofa and in the kitchen cupboards, while a smaller group, numbering thirty-six, resided on the top floor, where they made their residence in a forty-seven-year-old mattress and box spring that the farm owners, Sophie and Herb, used as their bed.

All of these rodents had free run of the entire old two-story farmhouse, including the basement where the potatoes, carrots, cabbage, onions, garlic and other vegetables were stored, along with the smoked hams and the smoked and cured summer sausages that hung from the overhead floor beams.

Food storage included the kitchen pantry on the main floor where there were various kinds of cheese, freshly churned butter and pasta, along with freshly baked loaves of rye bread and tasty buttered zwieback buns. The third floor had little in the way of food storage but was an envied place because it was warm during the cool winter nights. All of these furry residents lived in a bountiful haven with no sense of want or fear of impending dangers and changes.

These mice were pampered and accustomed to an easy life compared to the other colonies of mice that lived outside the farmhouse. Living inside was always warmer during the winter months, and even though the summer sun was known to become hot, these mice found the old farmhouse to be ever so comfortable.

These house rodents had shorter legs and smaller ears, and their fur was finer and much shorter in length than those who resided outside. The language of those that resided inside was softer, and they seemed to be less aggressive. All other mice referred to them as pampered, and as a result they were called 'Wimpy' because of their easy lifestyle.

Bolo, the senior rodent of the indoor Wimpy colony, managed all activities within the three communities of furry residents. He had organized workers whose responsibility was to bring food to the second and third floors, while others took care of the nursery where small hairless and blind babies wiggled and squirmed for food and attention. He had selected a reliable group to establish a warning system that could prevent injury or harassment from Marmalade or Fudge. He taught all of them about traps and grouchy humans, though none seemed to exist.

In the mattress and box spring on the third floor, there were many pathways to travel on and comfortable places for the residents to enjoy their lives. The mice could run throughout the entire mattress and box spring without making a sound. However, the only sound the mice would hear was Herb's nocturnal snoring, and, in a strange way, it comforted all in the room, including Sophie, Herb's wife.

This Wimpy group of mice never experienced difficulty, for there was always more than enough food to eat, the rooms were warm, and the housecats showed little interest in catching them. No one expected that their community would soon be challenged with chaos.

Chapter 13

THE BARN MICE

The mice that lived in the red barn surrounded by several corrals, a tall wooden silo and food storage bins were larger in size than the Wimpy mice that resided in the farmhouse. These mice had more muscular legs and larger ears and were extremely fast when they raced from place to place. Their fur was denser, and their noses and ears were constantly twitching as they smelled the air and listened for danger. Their language was similar; however, differences existed, and anyone gifted in Rodent language generally discerned a harsher accent. These mice had no known reason to fear or despise the privileged mice; however, it was evident that some prejudice existed if and when they happened to meet. These mice benefited from grains such as oats, rye and barley, as well as other tasty objects such as pieces of tanned leather that had once been part of old smelly harness straps. These mice were known as Barn Mice.

A census had never been taken of these mice, but a conservative estimate suggested that the ground floor and hayloft housed a minimum of three hundred to four hundred residents. The reason that the numbers were questionable was that many additional mice lived in and under several steel granaries next to the barn.

None of these mice had ever set a paw inside the farmhouse, and few Wimpy mice had visited the barn, even though they had spoken to each other.

Lazlo was the most athletic member of this group, with muscular legs that would power him as he ran from one end of the farmyard to the other. He could jump over sticks and stones in his path. Female mice swooned when he walked by, and many a tear was shed by a dreamy-eyed adolescent mousette. His best friend, Henny, was an extremely handsome yet dishevelled young mouse with a noticeable limp that mimicked the trousers of a youthful singer whose surname was Presley.

To say these mice had less class and culture would be totally unfair because they sang in choirs and quartets and actively participated in singing contests. To keep their lives exciting they invented daring games like provoking Rusty, a large grouchy red rooster, especially when they stole eggs from the hatching boxes where the next generation of chickens were being hatched. When the hens sounded the alarm, all hell would break out. The scene was similar to a buffalo hunt on the prairie during the 1800s. Rusty and his female admirers raced after the mice who had been stealing eggs. Before long, even the ducks were involved in chasing mice. Several inquisitive sheep usually wandered near to observe all the chaos, and soon they were bleating and running around the corral. No animals were seriously hurt, but it certainly provided excitement, as well as training for the mice that were getting ready for the July 1st races on the Brunzhoffa farm.

****

Each year, on July 1, the same scenario would play out on this pristine farm. At eight a.m., Sophie and Herb would leave the farm for a community day of activities in Thistle. In the front seat of their truck was a large basket filled with several loaves of fresh baked bread, sliced ham and two cans of salmon and two cans of sardines for Sophie to make sandwiches, several bottles of pop, a thermos of black coffee and mugs, two jars of homemade pickles, raw carrots, tomatoes and an onion. The remaining space was taken up with several type of cheese, two pies, frosted cupcakes and a pan of chocolate puffed wheat cake. It was a basket of extreme value.

Aside from the Slow Pitch Softball Tournaments, friends met at the sports grounds to participate in dozens of important contests like cheese tasting, pie and cake judging, and hotdog eating competitions, as well as sewing and knitting displays. Young calves and baby hogs were sold, while children played in the hot sun. Sophie and Herb had never missed this special day since they were children. This annual event was a significant milestone in their year and their lives.

Herb and Leo willing participated in the annual Horseshoe Tournament, but, as both men admitted, they had never won any games in forty years.

While the humans eagerly prepared for a fun day, the mice at the Brunzhoffa farm prepared for a day that they would remember.

****

The last group of mice living near the farm site survived in the fields just beyond the perimeter of the farm buildings. They were known as Field Mice. They were significantly larger than members of the Wimpy group of mice or the mice known as Barn Mice. These Field Mice had much larger legs, and their fur was much denser. Their language was similar, yet different from either the Wimpy group or the Barn Mice. All of them feared and respected Marmalade and Fudge and Oatmeal, the friendly Sheepdog who slept on the front porch. The only other potential enemies included the occasional fox or coyote sniffing the closed door of the chicken coop before resuming a nervous trot through the farmyard during moonlit evenings.

Of the three groups of mice, the Field Mice were the most aggressive and confrontational. From a distance it was difficult to differentiate whether they were rats or ... mice on steroids. They seemed to enjoy arguments, physical confrontation and verbal disputes.

If there was a morsel of food that the chickens or geese were dining on and a Field Mouse decided to take it, the confrontation was brutal. The sounds were usually loud, and feathers were usually strewn about. Even Rusty, the large red rooster, carried scars to prove the ferociousness of Field Mice. These hostile mice actually bit the sensitive noses of several hogs over disputes about food ownership.

It is difficult to comprehend that three groups of mice could be so different and yet communicate with each other.

Stumpy, the largest Field Mouse, had a booming voice that sounded like he had gargled with razor blades. He left little doubt as to who was in charge. He often sounded like a General giving orders to his troops during a fierce battle.

Hard as it might be to believe, Bolo, Laslo and Stumpy met shortly after Sophie and Herb left the farm for the Fair Grounds in Thistle. The three agreed that the sporting activities between the three groups were to be honorable.

The Wimpy group promised to provide a large round block of white cheese that Sophie had made and stored in her pantry in the cool basement. This block of smelly cheese was more valuable than any gold medal.

The major competition was an intense relay race from the windmill around the outhouse to the shortest scarecrow in the garden. A walnut was to be passed to a second mouse that would race it out to the rose bush half way out to the mailbox next to the roadway. After the exchange, the next mouse would carry the walnut from the rose bush to the roadway, and the next would bring it back to the hay wagon next to the barn. Then the next racer would carry the walnut to the water trough next to the sheep pen. From the water trough, another racer was to carry the walnut to the chicken coop door, and the next racer was to carry the walnut to the base of the tallest scarecrow in the garden. At that point there was a sharp turn to the right and a final dash for a hole in the concrete foundation of the barn. The mouse who made it through that hole carrying the walnut would be clearly the winner.

The only other rule was that each leg of the race was to be run by a separate member. NO mouse was allowed to run more than one portion of the race.

Bolo, Lazlo and Stumpy agreed that the race should go ahead as planned; after all, it was a bright sunny day and the owners of the farm were away.

Just before ten a.m., the three mice handed over their rosters of who were the eligible runners.

From the **Wimpy Colony**, the list of runners included:

Name	Age	Gen	Portion of Race
Maria	3 y/o	F	windmill to the shortest scarecrow in the garden
Pasco	3 y/o	M	from scarecrow to rose bush half way to the road
Haddy	3 y/o	F	from rose bush half way to the road to the mailbox
Patrizio	4 y/o	M	from mailbox by the roadway to hay wagon next to barn
Guido	4 y/o	M	from barn to the water trough by sheep pen
Manny	3 y/o	M	from the water trough to chicken coop door
Angelo	3 y/o	M	to the tallest scarecrow in the garden
Giuseppe	4 y/o	M	through the hole in the barn foundation wall

From the **<u>Barn Colony,</u>** the list of runners included:

<u>Name</u>	<u>Age</u>	<u>Gen</u>	<u>Portion of Race</u>
Nova	4 y/o	F	windmill to the shortest scarecrow in the garden
Hildee	4 y/o	F	from scarecrow to rose bush half way to the road
Cabre	3 y/o	M	from rose bush half way to the road to the mailbox
Marcos	4 y/o	M	from mailbox by the roadway to hay wagon next to barn
Ken	5 y/o	M	from barn to the water trough by sheep pen
Peter	3 y/o	M	from the water trough to chicken coop door
Edwina	3 y/o	F	to the tallest scarecrow in the garden
Rodney	4 y/o	M	through the hole in the barn foundation wall

From the **<u>Field Colony</u>** the list of runners included:

<u>Name</u>	<u>Age</u>	<u>Gen</u>	<u>Portion of Race</u>
Gus	3 y/o	M	windmill to the shortest scarecrow in the garden
Elmer	3 y/o	M	from scarecrow to rose bush half way to the road
Clifford	5 y/o	M	from rose bush half way to the road
Joseph	4 y/o	M	to mailbox by the roadway to hay wagon next to barn
Alfee	4 y/o	F	from barn to the water trough by sheep pen
Edwin	3 y/o	F	from the water trough to chicken coop door
Esther	3 y/o	F	to the tallest scarecrow in the garden
Frank	4 y/o	M	through the hole in the barn foundation wall

    Three dried walnuts from Sophie's stock in the basement of the house were selected as relay objects. They had to be small enough so the females could hold one in their mouth while running and still be able to breathe, yet large enough that they were not accidently swallowed by larger male runners.

    The umpires assigned to ensure that the race was run fairly were Bolo, Lazlo and Stumpy, along with sixteen other mice of good reputation.

Stumpy stepped forward and announced one last rule. "When you enter the barn to win, the winner MUST have the walnut in their mouth."

Bolo raised his front legs until there was silence. "AGREED . . . no winner will be declared unless . . . he or she has ENTERED the barn and IS CARRYING the walnut."

Before the race began, mice moved away from where the announcements were made because they wanted to be ready when their team members arrived.

At the front door of the barn hung a Swiss cowbell that had been worn by a milk cow in Switzerland. Herb used to ring it to summon the cows to the barn for evening milking. The umpires agreed that to start the race someone had to strike the bell. Wally, a Barn Mouse, was chosen for that honor.

After a great deal of stretching, jumping up and down, toe touching and exchanging of unruly trash talk, the competitors became silent and appeared ready for the race.

Chapter 4

A HEART-STOPPING RACE

The Swiss cowbell sounded, and a large and boisterous cheer urged the first three couriers into action. Nova leapt into the lead as Gus stretched into second place. Maria's heart skipped a beat when she saw that she was behind the other two mice. Her eyes narrowed as she began to run as hard as she could.

The sounds of cheering echoed between the barn and house as Gus overtook Nova when the three momentarily disappeared behind the outhouse, but, to the surprise of the crowd, Maria appeared in second place when the three neared the shortest scarecrow in the garden. Nova folded back her ears to streamline herself, but it was easy to see that Gus was clearly the stronger runner. However, the walnut exchange at the base of the scarecrow caused him to lose a few precious seconds when he allowed Pasco and Hildee to leave at the same time. Elmer was clearly angry at the poor walnut exchange and tried desperately to recapture the lost three to four seconds of the race.

The noisy crowd caused Oatmeal to leave the porch and walk to the back of the house to see what all the noise was about. Just then the three Olympians raced by, stirring Oatmeal into action. He barked loudly and began to chase Pasco, Hildee and Elmer. The crowd was too busy watching the race to scatter; however, Oatmeal's barking did increase the speed at which the three ran.

At the base of the rose bush, Clifford started to run but dropped the walnut. When he stopped to pick it up, Cabre and Haddy utilized their speed to run ahead of Clifford, who stumbled and fell. The walnut popped out of his mouth again and began to roll away, so he was forced to retrieve it before leaving.

The crowd was in a fevered state, and Oatmeal's continuous barking forced the runners to run faster than anyone could have guessed. Even Rusty got into the action by finding a perch on the hay baler, where he crowed continuously.

Cabre arrived at the mailbox; however, the walnut exchange did not go well, causing great anxiety to Marcos. The walnut seemed to be too large for his mouth.

From that point on, Cabre and Joseph were even, though Patrizio was clearly ahead. The crowd continued to cheer and started to run alongside as a sign of encouragement. This caused an enormous amount of chaos, with hundreds of mice running into each other. Several fist fights broke out as Patrizio arrived at the hay wagon. He ran as though his tail was on fire. Marcos eagerly followed, but Patrizio was clearly a better runner. Joseph gasped loudly as he tried to make up valuable time, while Guido lost valuable time when he started to run before he had possession of the precious walnut.

Alfee and Ken tried their hardest to move ahead, but Guido remained steadfast and started to run for the sheep pen. By now the crowd was totally out of control. Mice were running into each other, and those designated to run found it hard to concentrate on the next marker.

Oatmeal barked so loudly that he had to stop for a drink of water.

Edwina, a large-boned female with the reputation and demeanor of an angry wrestler, knocked over several dozen racing fans when she arrived at the door of the chicken coop just as Angelo was about to leave for the tallest scarecrow in the garden. Edwina purposely knocked him to the ground before leaving. Struggling to his feet, he gasped for breath and then momentarily dropped to one knee.

The race across the garden was destructive. Lettuce, cabbage, carrots and dill were destroyed and uprooted during the race toward the tallest scarecrow. While at the base of the large scarecrow, Patrizio elbowed his way into the crowd to whisper something to Giuseppe.

The crowd cheered and chanted the names of their heroes while the slippery wet walnuts were being exchanged. Suddenly Frank broke free of the mob, with Giuseppe and Rodney only two strides behind.

The mad dash for the hole in the foundation wall of the barn was a downhill race, without any barriers. The three racers focused upon one thing . . and that was to be first through the hole.

The pace of the race was beyond imagination. Even Oatmeal was unable to keep up. The crowd held its breath and stared at what happened next. Stride for stride the racers maintained their precious positions. Mice that were not careful were run over and stepped on by the crowd, including Oatmeal.

A major confrontation erupted when Rusty, the red-feathered rooster, stepped in front of Oatmeal. Suddenly colored feathers were drifting in the afternoon breeze. As Rusty limped to the side of the barn, several chickens decided to attack Oatmeal. The confrontation lasted a few seconds before several hens lay seriously injured.

At that moment there was absolute silence, heralding an impending life-changing catastrophe. Witnesses recalled seeing Frank tilt back his ears as he tried to narrow his body for the hole in the wall; however, his face with the wide walnut in it, jammed into the hole, and he was unable to move. As that happened, Patrizio moved a piece of wood that acted as cover over a hole next to where Frank's butt was sticking out. Giuseppe swerved and dived through the hole as Rodney ran into the rear end of Frank, who was hopelessly stuck in the tiny hole.

To say that life had little meaning after this incident was truly an understatement. Donnybrooks and fist fights broke out everywhere, and the chaos lasted for nearly an hour. The only way the members of the Wimpy Colony survived was to race to the farmhouse and squeeze through the many small openings in the basement foundation which only members of the Wimpy Colony could use.

Winning the race was of utmost importance; besides, Sophie's cheese wheel was retrieved and returned to the cool basement larder.

Those that escaped with their very lives were now safely huddled in their beds hoping to ease the high stress of the unforgettable afternoon. The farmyard was in an uproar until dark.

Canada Day was now officially over. What could possibly happen next year?

Chapter 5

HOME AT LAST

Sometime before midnight, the headlights of Herb and Sophie's truck bounced into the Brunzhoffa farmyard and slowly turned to face the southerly porch of the house.

"Where's Oatmeal?" asked Sophie. "He always meets us when we get home."

"Hope he's alright," responded Herb as he brought the truck to a gentle stop. After shutting off the engine and headlights, he walked to the back of the truck and stood in the darkness to relieve his bladder. Then he walked to the top of the steps and called to Oatmeal, who tried to stand but only lay there and yawned.

Meanwhile Sophie carried the large picnic basket into the house and turned on the porch light.

After ruffling Oatmeal's hairstyle, Herb entered the house. "Sophie . . . it seems to be extra quiet. I have a feeling that not all is well out here. The cows are not lowing to be milked, Oatmeal seems off stride, and the useless cats are nowhere to be found. I'd like to check the yard to be sure all is well."

After turning on the yard light, Herb grabbed the milk pails and went out to the barn. He was surprised that the cows were not there, so he rang the Swiss cowbell to call them to the barn. He rang it several times before they slowly and reluctantly approached the barn.

Another half hour passed before he returned to the house, and as he entered, he called Sophie. "This is weird. I had to call the cows several times before they came to the barn. They seemed reluctant to enter the barn for milking. When I milked the three cows, they did not give much milk. Their udders were full of milk, but I barely got any milk from all three of them. chickens laid any eggs. All the egg boxes in the hen house were empty. Something must have frightened all of them."

He paused as he handed a partially empty pail to Sophie. "As I walked across the yard, I noticed dozens of lumps of . . . things on the ground, everywhere. When I picked up several of them to see what they were, I was surprised to find that they were dead mice."

"Mice?"

"Yeah, dozens of dead mice, I tell you."

"What?" responded Sophie.

"Yes . . . yes, dead mice. Where they came from and what killed all of them is a mystery to me," insisted Herb. "I tell you something weird happened on the farm when we were away. Is it Full Moon . . . or what?"

"Maybe it was a small twister or strong wind."

"I found several injured chickens near the hay wagon and . . . Rusty the rooster was lying next to the barn. Some of his feathers are missing, and his legs are bleeding . . . and next to him were some of his feathers."

Herb reached for a flashlight and went outside to check on the dead mice. After returning twenty minutes later, he slumped on a chair in the kitchen and wagged his head. "There are dozens and dozens of dead mice, if not a hundred dead mice, in the middle of my yard. That has me stumped."

He lit a roll-your-own cigarette and watched the smoke rise to the ceiling. Ten minutes later he went upstairs, undressed and climbed into bed.

"Dead mice, huh?" muttered Sophie as she turned off the night light on the nightstand before rolling into bed.

****

For the next two days, Herb walked around the farmyard trying to solve the mystery. He telephoned several neighbors but did not find any answers to his dilemma.

Prior to the church service and following the sermon, he talked to every farmer in the parking lot, but no one provided any reasonable solution. No one else had that happen in their yard.

When he had finished his Sunday dinner, he went outside and spent the next two hours raking up mice carcasses and putting them in the burning barrel. When he had finished raking, he sat on the porch with a beer that Sophie had opened for him. He rolled another cigarette, lit it and leaned back in an old lumpy chair.

There must have been several hundred dead mice in the yard. That five gallon pail I collected them in was more than full."

When Herb had smoked his cigarette to an unmanageable length, he rolled a second one and lit it. As he exhaled, he muttered, "Cows that decided not to give their milk, dead mice everywhere, Oatmeal too tired to leave the porch and chickens refusing to lay eggs, not to mention a rooster that looks like he had the stuffing beat out of him and several injured chickens in the middle of the yard."

"Herb, don't hurt your brain over it. There must be a simple explanation."

"Dozens of dead mice everywhere . . . and the strange thing about it is that there were large ones, medium sized ones and small ones."

"Large ones?" asked Sophie.

"YAH . . . some as large as my fist," insisted Herb.
"As your fist? Are you sure they weren't rats?"

Chapter 6

THE VISA CARD

Little changed following the chaos of the Canada Day Race. Herb had a very restless night and complained all through breakfast about his sore back, and then, following lunch, Sophie walked out to the country road to check the round metal mailbox for an envelope bearing the much anticipated credit card. When she returned to the farmhouse, she sat on the porch and cut string beans and cut the tops off small carrots for supper, all the while planning how she would tell Herb about her new credit card.

Sophie realized that a guilty conscious was not an easy thing to live with. It was the first time in all her years of marriage that she had kept a secret from

Herb. It was not because she didn't trust him but because it was ... well, it was a lump in her chest similar to the time she, as a rotund child, had hidden those six colorful cookies in her dresser drawer when she had been told not to touch any of the Christmas cookies.

She remembered that they did not taste as good as they looked, and she was beginning to fear that using the Visa card, when it arrived, might not be as enjoyable an experience as it had originally sounded.

Thirteen days had passed since Sophie had applied for a Visa card, and then she found a brown envelope with a Visa logo on it lying in the mailbox alongside some colorful advertisements and the weekly community paper. As she looked at the envelope, she nervously adjusted her bib apron and then hand-brushed her hair that held her bun in place.

Looking both ways before reaching for the envelope marked Visa, she cleared her throat and giggled with glee. Taking it, she turned it over so that the sunlight would be on the printing. In the distance she could see Herb riding his old John Deere tractor near the slough, so she nervously opened the envelope.

There was the usual advertising scattered across the top of the front page, but her eyes were looking for her name and a statement that indicated she had been approved. She looked down the page until she read the following message:

Sophie Eleanor Lydia Brunzhoffa,
We are pleased to have you as a valued customer and look forward to assisting you with your future purchases. Just be sure to sign the back of the card and tend to the card so it will not be lost or stolen.

After reviewing your income, we are pleased to grant you a three hundred dollar credit limit. Should you require additional credit, please do not hesitate to contact our office by mail, or telephone during office hours. Our telephone number is 1-800-233- - - - -.

The signature at the bottom of the page was signed by a person who obviously had difficulty writing, for the name was illegible and appeared as a careless scrawl from a young child.

Sophie read the contents of the letter several times as she slowly scratched Oatmeal's head. Placing the envelope on the 12-inch black and white television, she stepped into the kitchen to prepare supper.

Sometime later, Herb drove into the yard with his dusty tractor and shut off the engine. He washed his hands in the water tank that the cows drank from and wiped his wet hands on the legs of his overalls. Then he reached for Oatmeal's ears as they walked toward the farmhouse.

"You're an old hairy-assed hound, but I love yah," he said to Oatmeal as they climbed the stairs of the porch that led into the house. When the screen door slammed behind him, Oatmeal turned three times to the right and then once to the left before stretching out on the porch for a well-deserved nap; after all, being a guard dog is strenuous work.

After sitting down at the table, Herb started eating his dessert first but stopped when Sophie cleared her throat and adjusted her bib apron. "Herbert Andrew Brunzhoffa, stop eating your dessert first. You haven't eaten any supper yet, AND you have not said Grace. You're starting to act like a real heathen."

"Who cares? Dessert is the best part of supper," he said as he put the spoon he had used to taste the chocolate pudding back onto the table.

After Sophie sat down, she nodded at Herb, who bowed his head and gave thanks for the pork chops, mashed potatoes, green beans and carrots.

Somewhere during the meal Sophie leaned back in her chair and said, "You complain about your back every morning, and I think it is time for us to buy a new mattress." She paused to look at him to see his reaction to her statement before continuing. "You know what I think? You'll sleep much better if we had a new one and . . . and your back wouldn't hurt every morning."

Herb wiped his mouth with the back of his hand. "And where do we get the money for one of those newfangled mattresses?" he mumbled as he reached for the bowl of potatoes.

"Well, Cuthbert's Furniture Store has a sale this month, and I . . . I would like to look at them, if that would be alright with you." She stirred her coffee before looking up at him.

"And where do we get the money for this here new . . . ah, mattress?" This time he wiped his mouth with a napkin.

"What do you think, Herb?"

"Hummm, pass the gravy." He always tried to sound stern and matter of fact like his mother used to when she spoke to Herb's father.

"I'll drive into Thistle tomorrow while the sale is on and bring one home. You'll see that you'll sleep better and your back won't hurt." She sipped loudly on her coffee before she continued. "Herb, you will sleep much better, and I'm sure both of our backs won't hurt."

"How much money are those things?" he asked as he plopped another spoon full of potatoes onto his plate.

"Herb, we've been married for over forty-seven years, and both the mattress and box spring sag like an old hammock. If one of us dies in that bed, the undertaker won't be able to get us out of it."

Herb could not resist chuckling at the thought of someone trying to lift his two hundred and fifty plus pound carcass out of a sagging bed.

Several moments of silence passed before Sophie continued, "What do you think, Deary?"

Herb cleared his throat as he placed another pork chop on his plate. He always cleared his throat when he did not know what to say next.

"Think about it," continued Sophie. "We sleep about eight hours out of twenty-four hours in a day, and that means we use that bed one third of our lives, so why not have something that helps us and . . . you'd sleep better, you know?" She reached for a freshly baked roll and placed it in front of his plate and then slid the butter dish toward him.

The entire evening was filled with a one-sided conversation as Sophie continued to speak about the different types of mattresses as well as colorful linen sheets, puffy pillows and bulky blankets that Cuthbert's Furniture Store was advertising in the local paper.

By ten o'clock Herb purposely nodded off to sleep to avoid more information which he did not want to hear. Had he heard about the credit card and what was to happen next, his sleep would not have been so restful.

Chapter 7

THE PRECIOUS PURCHASE

After breakfast the next morning, Sophie donned her fanciest dress, a pink floral-print pinafore, and then she pinned her hair up in a Gibson Girl style hairdo. She found some matching yellow clip-on earrings that were on a doily on her dresser and looked for her black shoes with the large black bow across the toes. Her heart raced and her breathing accelerated before she left the house to start the Ford pickup. Once Oatmeal was comfortably seated next to her, Sophie closed the door, revved the engine and placed the truck into first gear before starting down the lane toward the town of Thistle.

At the furniture store, she carefully parked the pickup truck and rolled down the windows for Oatmeal's comfort. She scratched his ears as she said to him, "Now you wait here until I get back. I shan't be too long, you hear?" He licked the back of her hand as she stepped outside and closed the door.

She entered the building just as one of the young clerks unlocked the front door. "Gooood morning, Lorraine," Sophie said as though she were singing a song.

Lorraine responded, "Good morning, Mrs. Brunzhoffa," as Sophie made her way to where the mattresses were and immediately sat on every mattress on display.

After she had wiggled her rump on each bed in the store, the proprietor asked, "Which one of these do you think you like the best?" He adjusted his bow tie and reached for the ballpoint pen in his shirt pocket. "All of these are on sale this month to make more room in our warehouse for some new couches and several 21-inch Zenith televisions."

"This one looks like it might be comfortable and . . ." she paused as she bounced up and down several times.

"Well, the best way to be sure is to lie on it for a few moments and roll to one side and then the other. Ask yourself: is it easy to get into the bed and easy to get out of it?" continued the proprietor.

After an hour of watching her try out all of the mattresses several times, the owner excused himself to get a cup of coffee. When he returned, Sophie smiled and pointed at the one she thought would be the best. At the counter, the owner filled out the necessary forms to complete the transaction and then turned to her and asked, "And how will you be paying for this, young lady?"

A large smile crossed Sophie's face as she handed him her Visa card. She was so excited that words did not come to her, so she watched silently as the card was placed in the imprint machine. Once she had heard it click several times, she managed to softly utter, "Oh, dear!"

"Please sign your name at the bottom of the page . . . and on the imprint sheet from the Visa card," said the proprietor.

As Sophie carefully wrote her name on the long line across the bottom of the order form, a smile crossed her flushed face because she was proud that she had stepped into the seventies by purchasing something large and useful with her new personal credit card.

A moment later the salesman said, "Thank you, Sophie, for your business. Do you want us to deliver it to your home?"

"Oh, no," she responded. "I have a truck you can put it into, and I'll take it home this morning."

After her precious purchase had been loaded into the back of the truck, the salesman reassured her that she had chosen the best mattress and box spring money could buy. He encouraged her by telling her that this mattress was just what would help her husband's aching back.

"This will make quite a difference to our sleep because our old sagging lumpy mattress needs to be replaced because it seems to hug you rather than support you. I'm planning to come back to purchase some sheets and a blanket in a week or two," Sophie said as she nervously searched for the keys that were somewhere in the bottom of her over-stuffed brown purse.

Before leaving town, Sophie purchased some fruit at Miller's IGA Grocery Store and then started the four-mile drive into the country. Nothing else occupied her mind, not even Oatmeal, who lay next to her on the front seat, nor the bag of groceries purchased to make dinner. All she could think about was the new mattress and box spring that would make sleeping more enjoyable. She tried to steer the truck safely down the gravel road and only once, for a few seconds, did she lose her driving concentration when her right hand stroked Oatmeal's ears.

The road was dusty and very bumpy at times, but a quick glance into the rear view mirror assured her that all was well. She stopped by the side of the hay field where Herb was baling hay and walked into the field to give him a banana and an apple for lunch. Oatmeal bounded over the newly mowed hay to meet his master, who had been riding the faded green John Deere Model AR tractor.

Herb bent down to scratch Oatmeal's ears as he walked toward Sophie and the half-ton truck. Moments later, Herb removed his straw hat and wiped the sweat from his brow with the sleeve of his red plaid shirt. Finding a small candy in his overalls, he placed it into Oatmeal's mouth. When Oatmeal recognised the taste, he immediately ran several feet away to eat it in private.

"Oh Herby dear, I'm so excited about the new bed. Come and see it. We'll sleep so much better tonight. I bought it today at Cuthbert's Furniture Store, so come and see it. Hurry, my dear. Come and see it." She tugged gently on his sleeve.

She grasped his large calloused hand and eagerly pulled him toward the truck while, with his other hand, he took his handkerchief from the back pocket of his overalls and wiped his brow.

"Sure is hot today. Should be done making hay in a couple of hours," he said as he willingly followed her to the truck. Before he actually looked at the purchase in the back of the truck, he stopped and rolled a soft lopsided cigarette and lit it with a match, not because he needed it but to build the suspense for Sophie.

"Well, what do you think, Herb?" she asked as she ran her hands over the dusty plastic cover of the mattress.

"Nice color, I suppose," he said as he allowed the smoke to flow from his open mouth and nostrils.

Oatmeal nudged him with a stick that he had found, so Herb tossed it into the ditch and called "Go find him." Eagerly, his shaggy friend searched for this useless treasure in the long grasses. Oatmeal was not easily distracted, but in this case there seemed to be several large field mice nervously scurrying under the grasses, so he followed their scent, and the chase was on. The stick was soon forgotten.

Oatmeal was eager to catch one of these furry trespassers so he could bring it back to his master, but there seemed to be so many of them and they were moving in so many directions. Busy dogs are certainly not aware of time when involved in a pleasurable hunt, so he did not hear Sophie's call or Herb's whistle.

Herb returned to his tractor, and Sophie drove the truck toward the farmyard. Once in the yard, she tried to back it up to the front door and bumped into one of her newly planted bushes. She stood by the front door and thought about how she could get the purchase into the house and up the stairs and what she should do with the old bed set. She tried to reassure herself that this would be easy, but, after tugging, lifting, sighing and grunting, she sadly abandoned the task. Then she telephoned her sister-in-law, Edna, to invite her and her husband over for supper.

At 5:30 p.m. Edna and Leo arrived for supper as Herb rode his tractor into the farmyard. While the men visited next to the truck with the mattress and box spring on it, Sophie was frying chicken and Edna was setting the table.

When they had eaten, Leo and Herb went to the second floor to bring the old mattress down the stairs, but the narrow staircase and sharp turns at the top of the stairs made the move almost impossible. When they set the mattress on its side, the rodents that were inside were tossed about as if they were in the rinse cycle of a washing machine. Everything they had, food, bedding, young offspring and padded roadways, collided in a dusty wind whirl. It was impossible for them to see and breathe, so all they could do was to try to grab the stuffing and hope that soon this nightmare would end.

As the men slid the mattress down the bumpy stairs, the resident rodents tumbled into each other as they tried to protect their offspring and survive the endless swirling and swaying. At the front door, the men dragged the mattress out onto the porch and set it up against the outer wall of the house just as the screen door slammed loudly behind them.

"Do you want to take the new mattress upstairs before we bring the old box spring down?" asked Leo, who wiped his forehead with the back of his hand.

"Naw, there's not enough room upstairs, so let's get the box spring down next," insisted Herb.

The box spring was more difficult to remove from the bedroom, and maneuvering it around the narrow staircase was almost impossible because the sides were rigid, not like the sides of the old saggy mattress.

When the men wrestled the box spring down the stairs, many of the mice escaped into the furnace duct and holes in the baseboards, and as a result few mice experienced the wild bumpy ride down the creaky stairs.

Within the hour, the men had moved the new bed up the stairs and set it onto the bed rails so Sophie and Edna could spread the sheets on it and reset the blankets. While they did, Leo and Herb tossed the old mattress and box spring into the back of the truck and closed the tailgate. After smiling at each other, they retired into the living room to sit in stuffed chairs and share a pint of ale.

When the sun was touching the western horizon, Leo stood to his feet, stretched, yawned and said, "Well, I'm still here, so let's get rid of that old bed that's in the back of your truck."

When the men had closed the doors of the truck, Herb drove it on a bumpy road next to a fence line at the back of his property. Long reeds of grass gently tapped the bumper and headlights as several grasshoppers jumped up onto the windshield. Sometime later, they crossed a shallow creek that was flowing over small round rocks; these provided a solid roadway for the truck. When they came to a point where four fences met, Herb backed the truck up to a pile of junk containing metal and wooden objects. Here Herb and Leo rolled the mattress and box spring off the back of the truck.

The box spring bounced and fell across several large pieces of metal from an old piece of farm machinery, and the mattress fell onto it and seemed to gasp as though it had just died.

When Leo was about to step out of the box of the truck, he spotted several mice scurrying about in the back of the truck. "Hey, Herb, we have some guests riding with us. Give me a moment to use this broom to sweep them off the truck."

Six surprised and reluctant rodents tumbled through the air after Leo had swept them off the truck. Most fell onto the fallen mattress, but the rest were swept into the long grasses that surrounded the junk pile.

"I hope they have a good life out here," laughed Herb as they drove across the creek and started for home."

The headlights of the truck shone against the spindly strands of long grass and weeds as grasshoppers continued to jump up onto the hood of the truck as it bounced over the primitive roadway. When they arrived at a gate that kept animals in the pasture, Leo stepped out of the truck and opened it until Herb had passed through.

Chapter 8

LIFE BRINGS CHANGES

Meanwhile, the silence surrounding the junk pile was deafening. The mice that were inside the mattress and box spring when it had been tossed were extremely frightened, confused and unable to breathe because of the dust. They lay desperately quiet and dazed.

Those that had been swept into the dark grasses from the back of the truck were bruised and fearful of moving, so they remained silent, waiting for death. The cool night air enveloped them as they huddled in the grasses.

****

At ten o'clock, Leo and Edna decided to go home. After they left, Sophie rushed upstairs to look at her bed. With the box spring and mattress in place, Sophie primped her hair with both hands, removed her apron and sat on the edge of the bed.

"Oh Herbert," she called. "This is so wonderful. Your back will feel so much better in the morning. I just know it. Please come upstairs and try it. Take my word for it. Oh, this is so good." She lay back and stared at the paint that was peeling on the ceiling. She folded her hands a though she was about to pray and giggled like a young school girl.

Herb went upstairs and slumped into an old stuffed chair next to the window. It was obvious he was fatigued from a full day of work and the furniture moving. "Well, I'm glad that's all done. Now how much did it cost?"

"Don't worry, Herb. We have thirty to forty-five days to pay for it, and if we don't like it, we can take it back. Thirty days, you hear, to use it free. What do you think?"

He unlaced and removed his high-top boots, leaned back and wiggled his toes. "Should have bought new socks 'cause this one has a hole in it," he said as he looked down at a large hairy toe protruding from the irregularly shaped hole.

"Was it more than $50 for the mattress and box spring?" he asked, knowing it would be much more. He rolled a cigarette and lit it with a wooden match he found in his pocket. Smoke curled from his lips and to the ceiling as he waited for her answer.

When Sophie was slow to answer, he asked again, "How much did it cost, my dear?"

"Don't worry, Herb. We have thirty days to pay for it . . . 'sides, it was on sale."

"I wonder why you don't want to tell me how much it cost," Herb mumbled as smoke continued to flow from his nostrils and mouth.

Both of them went downstairs to sit on the porch for a while. He watched lightning cross the eastern sky, and somewhere coyotes called to each other through the darkness.

"Herb, look at all the twinkling stars. I wonder if they see us . . . or hear any of those coyotes. Isn't it wonderful to be alive, Herb?"

Herb was unsure what to say, so he sighed loudly and used his thumb to shake the ashes off his cigarette before raising it to his mouth.

****

Life was good for everyone except the mice that were still in the mattress and box spring that lay in the cool night air on the junk pile out on the back forty. They had never experienced such chaos or the cold night air. With their world so badly shaken, they huddled together to keep warm, and the older mice mourned those that were missing. They had heard about disasters and violence like this, but this was worse than any of the mice could comprehend. It included missing friends and family, personal injuries, loss of food and loss of the lifestyle they had known.

****

The rising sun's rays slowly reached across the farmyard as Rusty the red rooster jumped up onto the hay wagon. The large arrogant red rooster announced to all residents that a new day was about to begin. His shrill voice made it difficult for anyone or any animal to continue sleeping after he had performed his morning aria. Afterward he flapped his wings for several moments to show he meant business. He had a way of intimidating all fowl as well as the cows and the sheep.

The sun warmed the side of the white two-story house as Herb continued to snore,

Meanwhile, Angelo and Patrizio searched the entire house for Giuseppe as wild rumors of death and separation swirled throughout the rodent world. There was no time to rest because everyone on the main floor was trying to make sense of the upheaval. Their greatest grief resulted when deceased mice were found at the bottom of the stairs and on the front porch of the house.

Grief and fear ruled their fractured world.

Chapter 9

PLEASURE AND PAIN

Sophie slipped into her plaid housecoat and put on her fuzzy pink slippers before opening the window blinds. Fresh warm sunshine invaded the room moments before Herb grunted loudly.

"How's your back, Herby, my dear? You'd better enjoy it because as of today all that back pain is officially gone." Her words were sung as a child's nursey rhyme.

Herb groaned as he pulled the covers over his head. "Life does not get easier as you age. Now I have dozens of dead mice to think about, a wife who insists my back will improve if I buy a new mattress on sale, a dog I care about who seems too tired to walk about when I call him, cows that quit giving milk because something frightened them, a bed to pay for and I don't even know how much it costs . . . and goodness knows what else."

"Did you sleep well?" Sophie asked as she searched for her wire-rimmed glasses on the night table and then exhaled on the lenses before wiping them with a linen handkerchief.

When Herb sat on the edge of the new mattress, he insisted that he wanted his old mattress back because this one was too much money. He muttered about it just to keep Sophie on edge, so she sighed loudly, put her hands on her hips and went downstairs. She made the coffee extra strong because she felt that if he had something else to complain about, he would forget about the cost of the mattress.

Herb shaved as Sophie stirred the pancake batter. Moments later, she sifted more flour into the batter and added another egg. When Herb put his razor on the edge of the sink, he wiped small amounts of excess shaving cream from his face with a towel and started for the kitchen.

As Herb poured homemade syrup over his pancakes, Sophie asked, "Well, Herb, how is your back? Is there any pain?" to which he responded, "The only pain I have is in my wallet . . . but yes, my dear, I hate to admit . . . I don't feel as stiff and sore as usual."

Sophie poured coffee into his favorite cup and leaned over and kissed the bald spot on the back of his head.

"You're a good wife," Herb said as he chewed on a piece of pancake . . . "but you'd be even better if you told me how much this cotton-pickin' thing cost me." There was a sound of bridled frustration in his voice.

"More coffee, dear?" asked Sophie as she carried the coffee pot to the table, cheerfully ignoring his questions.

Oatmeal nudged Herb's leg, so Herb handed a piece of pancake to his special friend.

****

Mice know nothing about time, but what they did know was that something had turned their world upside down, causing injuries, death and the loss of most of their food supply. As far as they were concerned, chaos and destruction were everywhere. Most pathways were blocked by large lumps of mattress stuffing, and two large holes had now appeared in the walls of the mattress. The box spring was twisted, and the dust in the tunnels made it difficult to breathe.

Bolo, their leader, had survived the tumbling but had an injury to his hind leg, yet he made every effort to calm his fellow rodents.

When morning light appeared, he organized a search of the mattress and box spring to determine how many mice had been injured and if any were dead. There was great sadness when the search parties found the total destruction of the rodent nursery. No babies had survived. Bolo immediately announced a day of mourning in memory of those that had died. Sadness gripped every heart.

Giuseppe tried to make sense of the upheaval, but the separation from his friends was particularly difficult. They had been together every day for as long as he could remember. He rushed through the damaged pathways and broken springs, hoping to find Angelo and Patrizio even though he knew they lived on other floors.

An organized search inside the mattress and box spring took some time, and when all corners had been searched, all who had survived gathered in what was once the nursery. Out of the original thirty-six mice that had made their home on the top floor of the farmhouse, only nineteen adults had survived. The rest of the group were missing and presumed dead. Many of them had been crushed on the stairway and on the front porch of the house.

"I need not tell you that everything has changed," said Bolo as he leaned against a lump of mattress stuffing. "If we are to survive what has happened, we MUST make every effort to work together. First . . . I will try to make sense of what we are facing. Please be patient with each other and . . ." His voice cracked, tears welled up in his eyes, and for several moments he could not continue.

Later Bolo went out the side hole of the mattress and cautiously looked around. It was colder than what he had ever experienced, and everything appeared very strange. Even though the sunshine encouraged them to come out, Bolo was fearful and reluctant to let any of them go anywhere. They were used to hearing Herb snoring and certainly were not intimidated by Sophie's snuffling, but the new sounds they had heard during the night and what they saw in the daylight greatly intimidated all of them.

Bolo assigned the residents to bring the dead to the entrance/exit holes in the side of the mattress so they could be taken out and buried. He encouraged them to clean up their homes and fix the storage areas with whatever food remained. Bolo tried to assure them that all would be well, but in the end he harbored many personal doubts. He requested that, after they had completed their tasks, they meet in the former nursery to discuss what their next strategy should be.

As Bolo was about to call the meeting to order, he was overcome with grief by the absence of many of his friends. He wiped his eyes often to gain his composure and tried to appear strong.

"My wonderful friends . . . we have experienced great tragedy. Our families have been destroyed, some of our friends have been severely injured and others killed, and . . . our food supply has been ravaged. Our comfortable beds have been violated, and everything we enjoyed has been damaged. The most common questions that I hear are 'How will we survive?' and 'Will we be able to start our lives over again?'"

There was an uneasy ripple that passed through the nineteen mice that stood before Bolo. He wiped his eyes before continuing. "We have little choice but to make this our new home. There will be many things we do not like and may fear, but we have only two choices: either to rebuild and encourage each other or to scatter and perish . . . and the last one is NOT a good option."

By now the bright sun was warming the mattress that lay across the box spring, and new smells like flowers and green grasses were invading their meeting place, changing this event into a more positive one.

Bolo said that he would send some workers out of the mattress and box spring to search for food. Then he called for volunteers to search the area around the mattress and box spring for seeds and larvae that could be eaten, and he called for volunteers to rebuild the inside of their community.

"Half of you will search for food. Whatever food you find you may eat some if you are hungry, but half of it MUST be carried into the storage area of the mattress or box spring. We will not tolerate greed. While the food is being collected, others will prepare the storage and living area."

Sometime later, Bolo announced that Scully would be the overseer of the mattress and Topo would be the leader of box spring. Bolo spent more than an hour explaining what each one's responsibilities were and what they were obligated to do. He insisted that there were three priorities: first, to establish a warning security system or neighborhood watch; second, to assign duties such as food gathering; and third, to ensure that all citizens communicated with each other.

He concluded his speech with firm words: "Your obligation is to be the best citizen you could possibly be. The last thing we need are complainers, grumblers and lazy mice. Things are desperate, and we all need each other to survive."

When the warm sun settled in the west, the night air suddenly became cooler and unfriendly, especially when all the furry residents heard a loud screech of an angry animal outside. They crowded together into a group and tried not to move. Eventually some fell asleep, while others pulled their family members closer to themselves.

The next day was difficult for those assigned to search for food. By noon, all that had been collected were strands of grass seeds, several green leaves and two dead grasshoppers. The remaining hours in the daylight were spent huddling together.

Day after day the reluctant group searched for and carried seeds and leaves of grass into the mattress while others cleared pathways to travel on. At the end of each day, all were hungry, exhausted and in need of sleep.

Several days later, Bolo called a meeting to order and then watched as several mice helped the eldest of the group to the front to speak. Everyone knew who Liam was, so there was no need to introduce him to the group.

Liam was the oldest mouse to have survived, and everyone respected him for his kindness. He sat on a wad of packing, cleared his voice and brushed his grey whiskers. He began with, "As all of you know, I am the eldest of all of you and have lived through many things in many different places. Many mice laughed at me when I warned all of you that one day calamity would strike and things would change, not as we would like but in terrible ways. I have lived through years of plenty and good times, but it is now that we must work together. Many of my friends were killed or lost, and food was difficult to find — much like it is now."

He took several large breaths and wiped his mouth before continuing. "I came to the Brunzhoffa farm a long time ago. Before that I lived in a country far from here. Back then, bad times caused the residents to leave everything we owned, and that is when great dust storms darkened the sky. Cows starved, horse ran away, and the people who owned the farms moved away. We lost everything, including hope."

He coughed loudly before continuing. "My brudder and schwester and I happened to hide in a large box of clothing in the farmhouse owned by some humans named Vanderkruk. They always made the most wonderful cheese and never used traps to frighten or kill any of us. Then one day, the large trunk we were hiding in was loaded into a two-wheel cart and taken for a very long ride. The trunk we were hiding in was dark and was handled very roughly, so we were very afraid, unt . . . yah."

Liam paused to gather his thoughts before resuming his talk. "We traveled for days. We were scared and worried that we would never stay alive. In the darkness we eventually found and ate cheese and bread that had been stored near the top of the trunk. We were fortunate that we did not starve."

Liam told about the weeks of isolation and fear. Then one day the lid of the trunk was opened to fresh air and sunshine. One of the Vanderkruks reached into the trunk to take some food, and as they did, my brudder and I climbed out of the trunk, but before our schwester could escape, the lid was closed. So Ari and I escaped into the bottom of the vagon where we hid among the farm tools and coal. Ari, my brudder, and I found a mattress at the bottom of the two-wheel cart, and fortunately there was a small hole that we crawled into just before it was unloaded at a farm. We had no idea where we were or how long it would be until we would be safe again, but we took courage and tanked our Creator for helping us, unt . . . yah."

"Did you ever see your schwester again?" asked Yenny.

"No, ve never did find our schwester."

"My last part of this speech will be a surprise to all of you. After all those weeks, we found ourselves on the second floor of a warm house. So take heart, because tings will soon be better if we are patient."

When Liam had finished his speech, the remaining rodents rushed forward to hug him.

Chapter 10

NOW WHAT?

All the resident rodents living in the basement and on the main floor of the farmhouse were shocked when they discovered that those that lived on the top floor were missing and some of their bodies had been found on the front porch. They remembered hearing loud noises but had hidden during the ruckus, so they did not know what had happened.

Some speculated that the Field Mice had returned to continue the confrontation and donnybrook following the relay race. Many of the older ones insisted that all this racing and tomfoolery had incited an all-out war, and many speculated that it would never end. More conservative mice pointed out that had there been an intended war, the Field Mice would not have started on the top floor but the basement because of the food stored there.

Angelo and Patrizio were devastated at the loss of their bosom buddy. They ran from basement to top floor several times, but all they found on the top floor were a new mattress and a new box spring. There were no holes in the box spring or mattress, and the room was quiet. With no sign of Giuseppe or any of his family members, Angelo hid under the rug and sobbed because of the ache in his heart.

****

Meanwhile out in the grassy field, Giuseppe was busy helping the volunteers gather seeds and grubs when a large shadow suddenly appeared overhead and, in an instant, the sharp talons of an owl grasped one of the adult mice and carried it off before any of the group knew what had happened. All they remembered was the dark shadow and the screams of their friend before all went silent. They tried to follow the owl, but soon it was out of sight.

Terror struck Giuseppe's heart as he ran to find Bolo. Eventually Bolo gathered the group and reminded everyone that dangers were real and it was their responsibility to set up a warning system. "Remember that danger is living among and over us."

Days turned into weeks, and soon heavy blue clouds arrived and the breezes began to sting those that remained outside for extended periods of time. It was an unusual time for the terrorized aliens. They lived with fear of the unknown because everything was vastly different from what they remembered.

Silent snow fell during the night and covered the old mattress and box spring. The rodents were reluctant to go outside to search for food because they were surprised to see large round white objects similar to the mattress stuffing floating overhead and falling from the sky. At first they feared it, but soon they discovered that it was not a threat. Eventually they remained inside because of the extreme cold.

Day after day it snowed, and soon snow covered everything in sight. The temperature dropped to a point where the rodents thought they would perish if they went outside. Their greatest challenge was to keep the newborns warm in the nursery. Food was rationed because finding more seemed impossible. Fortunately the mice had gathered sufficient food to fill one of their storage rooms in the mattress and one in the box spring.

Meanwhile, some of elderly residents passed away. However, a new generation emerged and grew up expecting that everyone would continue to provide food and protection for them. They reluctantly gathered food and seldom cared for the ill and dying.

****

Months passed, and one morning Giuseppe approached Bolo. "Every morning as the sun is rising, I hear a strange sound in the distance that I've heard before, but . . . I don't know what it is. Have you heard it?"

Bolo narrowed his eyes, shook his head and said, "No, Giuseppe. I'm sorry. What is it like?"

"It is like a loud cry, but it seems so far away. Some mornings I can't hear it, but some cold mornings it is very clear. I know I've heard this sound before, and I'm sure you have heard it too."

Many days passed, and soon the larders were empty. Eventually, the sun warmed the surrounding area, and the snow began to disappear. It was replaced by fresh blades of grass and colorful wild flowers. Larks and Red-Winged Blackbirds arrived, as did the colorful Mallards and brown hens, along with huge Canada Geese. The sounds around the slough were almost deafening. Life became more bearable for the very thin residents.

Liam and many of the older mice died in their sleep; however, the new nursery was busy with pink naked squirming babies, and peace and cooperation became the norm.

Late one afternoon, there was an object moving near the box spring. It stopped near one of the small holes of the box spring. The object's tongue moved from side to side as it seemed to be searching for something. Its eyes did not blink but continued to stare into the narrow hallways of the box spring, and it looked as if it were looking for prey.

Chapter 11

UNKNOWN DANGER

The mice were not aware that they were being stalked by an enemy whom they knew nothing about and could never fight. The bull snake, a meter-long non-venomous constrictor, moves silently and enjoys mice, gophers and other small animals for its meals. With no experience in dealing with such a deadly enemy, the mice in the mattress and box spring were extremely vulnerable.

The reptile cautiously entered the box spring and moved confidently through the hallways of padding, following the odor leading it to prey. Occasionally it stopped as it flicked its black tongue from side to side. Its unblinking eyes studied the hallways within the mattress, turning suddenly to the left as it entered the nursery. There it found two mothers, who were so surprised that they stood still and accepted their fate.

Once the nursery had been devastated, the snake followed the scent of other mice. Unknowingly, Caleffi stepped in front of it. Caleffi shrieked loudly as a warning to the others but was suddenly grasped.

Soon all the mice began running to avoid the enemy; however, Caleffi was never seen again.

The community was destroyed by the destruction of the nursery and the death of Caleffi. Their fears were escalating, and many of the younger mice were inconsolable because Caleffi had been a pillar of strength to everyone. Bolo and Scully tried to calm their fears and did what they could to close the holes and seal their residence from other invading enemies.

The unfortunate thing was that the snake coiled up in the warm sun, on the ground next to the mattress. It became obvious, after several hours, that the snake had no intentions of leaving because it had found sufficient food to survive.

Bolo realized that their only defence was to plug the holes in the mattress to prevent the reptile from re-entering the mattress, so for the next few days the mice worked diligently to pack the large hole. The snake remained beside the mattress, but a week later the snake moved on, much to the relief of the mice.

****

Giuseppe had not forgotten about Angelo and Patrizio and often pined over the loss of his best friends, but he became active and participated in gathering food. Morning after morning, he stood at one of the entrances and listened for the strange and yet familiar sound he had spoken about to Bolo. It stirred his inner being whenever he heard it.

Meanwhile Angelo had given up hope of ever seeing his best friend. Time distorted his memory because he did not have a clue about what had happened so many months ago. His only option was to speak to the Barn Mice to see if they knew anything.

The Barn Mice claimed that they had no idea where to look and gave little assistance, so Angelo returned to his family in the farmhouse. He and his wife had a family to tend to, so much of his babysitting kept him from reminiscing about the good times with Giuseppe.

Patrizio's performances had ceased after the disaster because much of his time was also spent tending to his new family.

Chapter 12

THE FAMILIAR SOUND

Once again the evening air was becoming cooler, and leaves were beginning to fall, pressuring the food gatherers to work longer hours searching and storing food for the months to come. In the field they found wheat kernels, flax seeds, peas that a farmer had tried to grow, and seeds from crested wheat grass. Mice are herbivores; however, if desperate, they will eat ants, small bugs, snails and dead grasshoppers.

One morning, after the volunteers returned with seeds and grubs, Giuseppe approached Bolo again. "Sir," he said, "I have told you about a sound I hear every morning and the sound is in the distance. It sounds like someone calling for help. It's there early every morning just before the sun rises. I know I have heard this sound before, and it bothers me because I cannot tell what it is."

Bolo sat next to Giuseppe as he listened to him. "Yes, I remember you telling me this many times, but I don't hear it. Do others hear it too?"

"I don't know, but it is really clear some mornings and . . . I know I've heard it before. If you listened to it, maybe you would know what it is."

Just then several females started talking to Bolo about the need for a new nursery, so Bolo patted Giuseppe's back and went to attend to their request.

The next morning the ground was white again, and cooler air invaded the dumpsite and valley. The food gatherers reluctantly went outside, but by noon all of them were cold because they had to make their way through the snow-covered yellow and red leaves on the ground. Later that evening, while the citizens huddled together to keep warm, they became aware of a breathing and subtle sniffing sound.

At that moment, a black object appeared at the entrance of the box spring, and then a paw started to scratch at it to make the hole larger. Most of the citizens escaped through another opening and made their way to the mattress which was above them. When they arrived, they realized that the nursery was now vulnerable, so they scurried outside and made noise to distract the searching enemy. After several close calls, the citizens escaped, and the coyote lost interest and trotted away.

Now the priority was to seal the holes from enemies and to do something to keep the place warm at night. They worked very hard for several days, and when they met again, it was dark and they were exhausted and fearful. They plugged the entrance with dead leaves and small twigs.

Bolo tried to calm their fears, even though he realized that survival in this hostile place was almost impossible. But he knew that giving up was not an option, so he recommended searching for food every third day rather than every day. He hoped the enemies would not come by every day.

As the meeting was breaking up, Giuseppe once again told Bolo about the sound he heard just before sunrise, but Bolo was too busy to attend to Giuseppe's story.

A week later, several citizens were scrounging for food when they stopped next to a tree that had been felled by a beaver. They watched from a distance as the large animal waddled down into the water that had an icy crust on it. When the beaver was gone, they rushed over to taste the woodchips and found that some of them were tasty, so they returned many times and carried the wood chips and bark into their larders.

On one of their return trips, they were met by a large lumbering animal that seemed to care less about them, so they scurried under a log and waited until this obnoxious-smelling beast had passed. The obnoxious odor was terrible, and the black and white animal that carried it eventually shuffled off. Little did they realize that the odor of the skunk was effective in keeping snakes and coyotes away from their home.

One extra cool morning, Giuseppe went to Bolo's residence and begged him to come and listen to the strange noise he had told Bolo about. Reluctantly, Bolo followed Giuseppe to the top of the mattress. At first Bolo was perturbed by the story of a ghostly sound that was familiar to Giuseppe, but as the sun was about to rise, Bolo suddenly stood still and held his breath as he heard the familiar sound in the distance. The sound was certainly familiar to Bolo, who turned his ears westward to increase his ability to hear more effectively.

When the sound ceased, Giuseppe stared at Bolo. "Sir, what is that sound? I've heard it before. What is it, sir?"

"I know that sound too. It's the sound of . . . an . . . an animal . . . could it be Rusty the red rooster that lives on the Brunzhoffa farm? If it is, then we are not far away from where we lived. If it is, maybe we could find our way back home to the farmhouse."

Both of them stood in silence for a long time before Bolo turned to look at Giuseppe. "Giuseppe, please don't tell anyone about this sound. It will be our secret because I need time to think about this. DO NOT speak to anyone about this. Do you hear me . . . no one, you hear? I will see you here tomorrow morning so I can hear the sound again."

The next morning the valley was filled with fog; however, the sound was the same as before and lasted only a few moments. "Do you have any idea where it came from?" asked Bolo as he strained his eyes to see any landmarks on the distant horizon.

A week passed, and every morning Giuseppe and Bolo stared at the horizon. They finally agreed that the sound seemed to come from a dark clump of something in the distance which they suspected were trees.

One day Giuseppe and Bolo made their way to the creek, which had ice on the edge of it. Giuseppe walked on it for a few moments, but when his feet suddenly became wet, he rushed to the shore where Bolo was anxiously waiting.

"We'll never be able to cross this water," said Bolo as he heard a deep voice behind him.

Turning suddenly, he stared at one of two beavers that were looking at them. Bolo wanted to run because of the size of these animals and the size of their front teeth, but he realized that both he and Giuseppe were cornered, so they stood still.

"We've seen you before and are surprised by how little you are. Don't be afraid of us 'cause we won't hurt you. What are you looking for?"

Giuseppe tried to contain his fear as Bolo responded. "We are looking for a way to cross all that water."

"There is a tree that we dropped a few days ago, and it lays across the creek. You can cross the water over there," he said as he sat on his hind legs and pointed down the creek.

Bolo told them where they lived but could not tell them how they had arrived in this field. The beavers listened intently and led them to a large tree that lay on the ground. Beside it lay many nuts and acorns that had fallen out of one of the holes near the top of the tree. Moments later the beavers showed them dozens of pinecones that were spread across the snow.

Soon squirrels appeared and started to carry away the pinecones. Bolo and Giuseppe watched, and eventually all of the pinecones were gone.

Bolo whispered to Giuseppe, "We need to get back here as fast as we can because we need those pinecones and nuts in our larder."

Several weeks later, all larders were full of seeds, wheat, dead grasshoppers and grubs, tasty bark, grasses, acorns and nuts, which made the rodents confident that their survival was now assured.

Chapter 13

THE LONG AND BITTER COLD

Snow continued to fall in silence during the night, and by morning it was too deep for anyone to leave either the mattress or the box spring, so the rodents moved through the vertical entrance to eat with each other.

Days turned into weeks as the rodents survived on the food they had collected and stored days earlier. The nursery flourished, and it seemed that every few weeks there were more mouths to feed. Food supplies were becoming depleted when a blizzard struck the valley, leaving deep snow everywhere.

Then one late afternoon, three large field mice appeared at the entrance to the box spring. They forced their bodily frames into the entrance hole to get out of the cold and snow. All of them appeared famished and extremely exhausted.

Giuseppe and Bolo approached them. "I am Giuseppe, and this is Bolo."

"We got lost in the storm and have not eaten in several days. Can you spare some food for us?" said the eldest of the group as he dropped to his knees. They appeared gaunt and extremely hungry.

"We're running out of food too, but you're welcome to stay and eat with us," responded Giuseppe. After accepting Giuseppe and Bolo's invitation, the three field mice eagerly ate with them. They told Bolo and Giuseppe about their home in a haystack not far from here.

"It's just over the hill," said Edgar. "When we have a chance to travel, we'll try to make it home again, so you can follow us.

Giuseppe and Bolo were careful to share what food they had, but one day their larder was empty. Their three guests went outside and gathered what food they could to help replenish some of the food supplies.

****

A week later the three field mice thanked them for allowing them to stay during the storm. As the sun seemed warmer than before, much of the steel junk around their home was free of snow, and after a week of melting, the wet ground turned into soft mud, and several blades of green grass swayed in the cool breeze.

When all of the snow had melted, Giuseppe cautiously stepped outside to see what the world was like. He was amazed to hear Meadowlarks singing while bobbing their heads up and down as they sat on fence posts. He heard Robins chirping loudly as a warning to Red-Winged Blackbirds that flew over the marsh. In the distance, Crows cawed, and far overhead a hawk soared as if it were supervising spring activities.

Several days later, Giuseppe heard the strange sound he had reported to Bolo, and once again, his heart was stirred.

Giuseppe approached Bolo again and asked about the strange distant sound. Bolo agreed with Giuseppe, "Yes it would be nice to find it, and yes . . . maybe it will be near our old home, but who will go?"

"I have decided that we need to look for it," said Giuseppe. Maybe it's nothing, but maybe . . . it is something near our old home on the farm. I'll ask Tae and Malin to go with me, and when we find it, we'll return and tell you."

Bolo scratched his head and said, "Much as I am reluctant to admit it, that piercing sound might be . . . Rusty the rooster that crowed every morning when the sun rose in the sky. If you are willing to seek for that sound, regardless of what it is, then I will eagerly wait for your findings."

Giuseppe became emotional when he listened to Bolo. Tears flowed from his eyes when he hugged Bolo. "I have hoped for this day for a long time. We will find our old home."

Several days later, the three brave mice left the cheers of their families and friends and started for the creek where Bolo and Giuseppe had met the beavers several months earlier. When they arrived, they were surprised that the water was very deep and flowing very rapidly. The melted waters had turned the small creek into a torrent of cold swirling water.

Unable to cross the fast flowing water, they started to walk downstream as they looked for a place to cross. It was getting dark when they came across a tree that had fallen over the stream, and it was here that Giuseppe, Tae and Malin crossed to the other side and found a safe place to hide for the night.

During their frightening stay, they ate seeds as they looked up at the stars and speculated about what the moon was made of.

"Maybe it's made of cheese because it is round and very yellow," said Tae. "Like the cheese that our lady used to make."

"Wow, that would be so nice," responded Giuseppe.

"How come we can't smell it if it is cheese?" asked Malin.

"Don't know," muttered Giuseppe, as he closed his eyes to fall asleep.

When it was totally dark, the three snuggled together to keep warm

The next morning Giuseppe awakened to a shrill sound in the distance. He rushed out of the morning shadows to get his bearings so he could know where the sound was coming from. It was in line with some objects and trees in the distance, so he told the others to rise and eat so they could resume their journey.

By late afternoon they were passing a slough with hundreds of ducks and mud hens swimming on it while blackbirds argued over nesting sites. Tae was the first one to stop because he was tired and wanted a rest. Giuseppe agreed with Tae, and soon the three were squatted next to a fence post surrounded by several stones. It was a perfect place to stay for the night.

They managed to share some wheat seeds and flax seeds they found before crowding together for a restless sleep. Midway through the night, a strong breeze ruffled their fur, and eventually raindrops fell on them, so they were forced to look for another place.

Tae and Malin followed Giuseppe as he ran through the darkness seeking a safer place to hide. Large white sheets of lightning blazed on the other side of the creek, and the thunder seemed to shake the ground they ran on.

Giuseppe saw a bale of hay in front of him, so he called to his friends. When the three rain-soaked mice huddled at the side of the bale of hay, they were wet and exhausted. Tae burrowed into the bale so they could hide from that rain.

In the morning sunshine, they shared oat seeds from the bale of hay and licked their wet fur. Once they left the safety of the bale of hay, they passed a flock of woolly sheep, which ignored them, and then they scampered near several cows. Then the three continued running toward the side of a red barn where chickens and a rooster were scratching the ground as they searched for seeds. Sometime later, they made their way into the barn and hid beside several bales of hay and three sacks of oats.

"This is where we were living a long time ago. There is the large house, but how do we find our relatives?" asked Tae.

As he spoke, a large mouse scurried across the floor of the barn and disappeared behind several large wooden boxes. Giuseppe cautiously crossed the floor to where he last saw the large mouse. After taking a breath, he stepped through a hole in the barn wall. There before him were dozens of large mice, who stood still as they stared at the three aliens and then suddenly turned and scurried away.

"WAIT," Giuseppe shouted. "We mean no harm. We are mice and need your help."

A few moments later, two mice approached the three foreigners.

"Where have . . . you come from?" asked one of them.

"A long time ago we lived here in that farmhouse," he said as he pointed at the farmhouse. "Somehow we were taken to a foreign place where we almost died. We have come back, so don't be afraid of us. We are as afraid of you as you are of us."

All of them stood in silence and stared at each other.

****

Later that evening, after they had eaten, Giuseppe and his friends told the Barn Mice about all the upheaval in their lives and families. They told of their trip to this barn and the loud sound they always heard that attracted them to this place. When they were finished, Sampa, the Barn Mice leader, realized that the sound they remembered hearing was Rusty the red rooster who crowed every morning before sunrise.

Giuseppe wiped tears from his eyes as he said, "So this IS where we lived before we were . . ." His eyes continued to well up with tears, and he found it hard to speak.

They visited long into the night, and before they went to sleep in the barn, Giuseppe, Tae and Malin stood in the moonlight that entered the barn through a cracked pane of glass. They stared at the farmhouse as they tried to remember their former life. The pain of being so close to their relatives and past life was extremely difficult. They leaned on each other and sobbed until their eyes could not weep anymore.

The next morning the three were awakened by Rusty the red rooster. His shrill crow echoed from building to building as he stretched his neck and flapped his wings to welcome the sunrise. In a strange way, he was also welcoming Giuseppe, Malin and Tae home.

The three amigos spent the entire day rushing from building to building as they searched for clues about where they used to live. They went from granary to garage and from tool shop to the wood house where all the chopped wood was stored for the winter. They even stopped next to the outhouse and caused a stir among the ducks that were busy eating quack grass. They watched Oatmeal playing with one of the housecats and followed Oatmeal as he trotted to the farmhouse. After climbing the stairs of the porch, he circled several times before lying down.

Beside the house, next to a cracked basement window, they stopped because there was a familiar smell: freshly baked bread. Tae searched for a way to enter, and after cautiously moving the broken piece of glass, he squeezed into the small hole and turned to encourage Giuseppe and Malin. It took some time and much encouragement for the other two to enter the house through the broken basement window.

Once inside, they jumped down onto a sack of potatoes and scurried over to the furnace duct that had been an effective pathway to the main floor, but before running up to the main floor, they turned into a storage pantry where other vegetables and the dry summer sausage were hanging. As they stepped into the small vestibule, they were surprised to see several dozen mice.

When Giuseppe recognized them, he shouted, "IT'S ME . . . GIUSEPPE. I'M BACK. I HAVE BEEN GONE FOR A LONG TIME, BUT NOW I'M BACK. DO YOU REMEMBER ME?"

A moment later, all of those who recognized him rushed out and danced around the three arrivals. Eventually all of the mice from all of the floors were visiting with Giuseppe, Tae and Malin. It was such a wonderful reunion. Stories were exchanged as they embraced and hugged long into the night.

When Giuseppe asked about his best friends, Patrizio and Angelo, there was long silence before Giuseppe was told that both of them had left their families to look for their friend and those that had lived in the mattress and box spring on the upper floor. Sadly, they had never returned.

Filled with grief, Giuseppe told them of the sudden move that took them into the cold countryside. He told them about those that had been lost and killed. They spoke until morning.

Giuseppe was told about the new mattress and box spring and how things had been difficult until a new hole had been chewed into the mattress.

Giuseppe told them about his plan to return to the dump and bring the mice back to their home

The air was filled with the sounds of sobs and groans as Giuseppe grieved the loss of his two special friends and all the changes that had taken place.

Many were amazed at the bravery of Giuseppe and of those who came with him to search for their original home.

"What can we do to help?" asked Campen, who was the leader of those that lived in the basement. He was very stern but willing to listen to the plight of the three prodigals who had been lost and returned.

Giuseppe cleared his throat before he spoke. "Well, finding our way here was a challenge. Without the sound of Rusty's crowing in the morning, we would not have known where our home had been, and we would not have found this place. We need to have him crow every morning, noon and evening. That way we will be able to return to our new home and return with our families. Are any of you able to speak to Rusty, or is there someone who can convince him to help us?"

"Rusty is arrogant, fierce and not one to reason with. Often he chases ducks, hens, mice and cats. The only one he cannot boss around or scare is Oatmeal, who took several of his tail feathers off when he tried to attack him several weeks ago. He is more of an enemy than a friend to everyone on the farm," said Campen.

"What can we do?" asked Tae.

"He is big, strong and confrontational. He struts around the farmyard daring everyone to fight with him. Even Dolly the mare tries to stay out of his way. I'm not sure there is anything we can do to have him cooperate," said one of the older and more senior mice.

During the next week all suggestions to get Rusty to cooperate sounded good; however, acting upon them always ended up failing. In one of the planning meetings, Campen made a suggestion. "There is only one animal on this farm that Rusty does not tangle with, and that is Oatmeal. Rusty challenged Sophie by flapping his wings and jumping up at her face, and when she screamed, Oatmeal came to her rescue, pinned Rusty against the barn wall and tore out some of his long colorful feathers. For the next week Rusty was careful who he challenged because Oatmeal stays next to Sophie to protect her wherever she goes."

Lester raised his paw, and, when acknowledged, he began to speak. "Rusty was humiliated in front of all the farm animals, especially the hens, so he is cautious whenever Oatmeal is near. After a week we noticed that Rusty crowed whenever Oatmeal was out of sight, so what we need to do is keep Oatmeal out of Rusty's sight, and I know how we can do that. Oatmeal is a dog, and dogs like to eat, so when Sophie bakes a cake or some tasty buns, we can give some to Oatmeal and hide him in the basement of the house until we know Giuseppe and the others are well on their way home. After that, we'll keep Oatmeal out of sight so Rusty will start to crow again, so Giuseppe and the boys can follow the sound of his crowing back to the farm. What do you think of that?"

All were in agreement.

Following the meeting, Giuseppe talked with family members for hours. There was much to hear about and new family members to meet. It ended when both were too tired to continue.

Chapter 14

THE RETURN TRIP

The three visitors did not leave the farmhouse the next day as expected, but stayed because of the threatening weather. There was a week of heavy rainfall, and during that time, it hailed, so they were forced to postpone their departure. The weeklong delay became a month, and soon thick snow clouds gathered and the ambient air became cold. When snow fell during the night, returning for the three seemed next to impossible.

Snow fell frequently, and winter became very difficult, so the three travelers remained in the warm farmhouse because traveling would have been impossible. Days passed, and soon the three became comfortable with the food, the warmth and the comradery in the old farmhouse.

Those at the mattress and box spring junk pile were concerned that the three might have perished. It was a difficult time for those waiting for their return.

In early spring, three field mice, Edgar and his two traveling companions, arrived at the junk pile. Bolo met with them, and once again they thanked him for providing food to them during their plight through the snowstorm.

"We have come to invite you and your families to join our families at the haystack. There is lots of food, and it is warmer during the winter months . . . so why not move to where we are and join us?" asked Edgar.

Bolo convinced the members to move to be with the field mice at the haystack. "You heard them. They have food, and their place is certainly much warmer in winter than this mattress and box spring. If we expect to survive and give our youth a chance to grow, then we must consider moving."

"What happens if Giuseppe returns? He won't know what happened to us." asked Milton, Malin's father.

"It has been months since he left, and winter has come and gone. We have an obligation to move to save our families," insisted Bobo. A week later, the majority decided to move. Several days later, the box spring and mattress were empty.

Eventually, the warm sun melted the snow, trees began to bud, geese flew overhead to northern nesting sites, and daylight became longer. Again birds chirped loudly among the reeds and cattails next to the marsh. Several of the cows gave birth to calves, while young lambs played silly jumping games in the meadow.

****

The warmth of an early summer reminded Giuseppe of his goal to return to the mattress and box spring where all his family lived. He became restless when he heard Rusty crowing one morning, so he told Malin and Tae that it was time to return. They announced their departure to their farmhouse friends.

While it was still dark, Giuseppe, Malin and Tae hugged their relatives who lived in the farmhouse and some of the Barn Mice before starting on their return journey. Eager to return, they set a fast pace until they arrived beside the slough, where they were too tired to continue, so they rested. They listened to the crickets, frogs and grasshoppers before falling asleep for the night.

They left the next morning, and when the sun was high overhead, they rested near an ant hill before resuming their fast pace. Several hours passed before Giuseppe told them to find a secure place for the night. Tired from the long walk, the three slumped on some leaves while they looked up at the clouds.

They watched several hawks soaring and circling overhead and listened to the crows in the distance. They could hear cows lowing and a dog barking. They felt comfortable when the crickets chirped and grasshoppers buzzed in the long grasses.

"Now all we need is to hear Rusty's morning crowing to help us correct our direction," said Tae as he closed his eyes to get some much needed rest. As darkness claimed the grassland, the three mice rested to prepare for the remaining portion of their trip.

Little did they know that Herb and Sophie had cornered Rusty in the barn and prepared him for a visit from the clergy along with other guests, who were invited for Sunday dinner. Rusty's bright-colored feathers danced across the farmyard as the afternoon breeze taunted his colorful memory.

The mice in the barn and farmhouse were in a panic because they knew that Giuseppe, Tae and Malin would be listening for that shrill sound to use it as a sound beacon for their return to their home and for their future return trip to the farm with their friends and relatives. There was no way to find Giuseppe and tell him about Rusty's demise, so they could only speculate about what would happen.

The next morning, Giuseppe was surprised that he did not hear Rusty but urged the others to find something to eat so they could resume their trip. The day was long and the sunshine became very warm, but the three did their best to keep a steady pace, and by the end of the day, they were very tired and hungry. They found seeds and some grubs and eagerly sought sleep.

The following day they followed the shoreline of the creek and found part of the downed tree they had crossed when they were seeking the farm. While crossing the creek, Tae slipped and fell into the fast flowing water. Though Giuseppe and Malen followed the shoreline and spent hours looking for him, they never found their friend.

In the early morning light, a coyote chased Giuseppe and Malen from their resting sites. They ran as fast as they could, and eventually Giuseppe jumped into the water to escape; the water turned him over several times, but he did manage to escape. He called for Malen but did not hear him; nor did he remember hearing Rusty's morning call.

When the sun was high overhead, Giuseppe walked in the direction of the junk pile. When he arrived, it was quiet, and there were no mice. He entered the hallways and found them empty. Greatly distraught, he sat down and sobbed because it was too much to bear. He had lost two friends and all who had been his friends.

When the night breeze reached out and touched him, he moved inside to find some matting and covered up before falling asleep.

Giuseppe was concerned because he could not hear the sound of Rusty's crowing. Every morning, he listened for the sound that he had heard, and soon he began to lose hope of ever hearing it again.

Chapter 15

HOME AGAIN

Giuseppe decided to return to the place of his birth. What troubled him most was that he did not hear the crowing sound and often wondered if all was well at the farm.

Giuseppe carefully examined the walls of the mattress and box spring. Then he walked through the hallways and checked out the nursery and larders again, and when he found nothing, he was convinced that something drastic had happened to the mice. Lonely and despondent, he decided to leave for the farm.

Before leaving, he ate some seeds that he found on the ground. It was late afternoon when he neared the place where they had spoken to the beavers. He called for them but never heard any response, so he sought a protected place for the night.

Severe rain delayed his return journey, the wind became very strong, and leaves and branches rolled around him. The next week he searched for seeds and grubs, and when he had eaten, he felt stronger to resume his journey.

When the sun was overhead, he found a small branch that had blown across the water, so he decided to attempt a crossing. Giuseppe started to crawl onto a wet branch, and though it was slippery, he successfully hung onto several leaves and finally jumped onto the shore on the other side.

After he had successfully crossed the creek, he remained there for several days before deciding whether to continue on or return to the junk pile. It was a very difficult time for Giuseppe, who seemed so hopelessly alone. If he could have heard the crow of the rooster, he would have known what to do, but there was only silence.

Traveling alone was very difficult, and each night he hid at the base of a tree or in some bushes. Fortunately, he found some seeds and blades of grass to eat.

He traveled two more days and was beginning to think that he had lost his way. Climbing on top of a boulder, he scanned the horizon for a better view; seeing nothing, he was about to crawl down off the boulder when he thought he saw a barn and trees. It was well off his pathway but he surmised that he had lost his bearings.

He moved quickly so he could arrive at what he guessed was the barn. In the evening twilight, things looked very different because there were no cows, sheep, chickens or geese, but there were long grasses that seemed to have captured the entire farmyard. As he rested to catch his breath, he realized that there was no farmhouse, only a pile of burnt wood and a partially collapsed brick chimney. Large burned pieces of wood protruded from the basement, and the brick chimney presented a ghostly image that intimidated him.

He ran as fast as he could to the side of the barn and squeezed into a small hole in the foundation. The full moon glowed through the eastern windows of the barn, chasing darkness into the corners, so Giuseppe scurried to what he thought was a sack of feed, and there he remained for the entire night.

Early the next morning, Giuseppe was awakened by the sound of mice running across the wooden floor. When he blinked his eyes to focus upon them, he realized that there were dozens of mice, so he stepped into the morning light and called to them. "I am a friend of Sampa. Is he still here?"

After some time, Sampa arrived, and when he recognized Giuseppe, he was glad to see him, so he invited him to enter a labyrinth of tunnels in and under the barn. There they offered him barley and ground oats and welcomed him into their world.

"Why does this place look so different from what I remember?" asked Giuseppe. "Nothing looks the same. What has happened?"

"The day you left for your home, everything changed. The lady in the house and her husband decided to use Rusty for Sunday dinner, and that is why you never heard his crowing again. A few days later, the house burned down, and the people moved. They returned to sell the sheep, cows, chickens and ducks. Strangers came and took the horse and her colt, which had now grown into a large horse. Eventually only the lady of the house came by with Oatmeal, but when the snow arrived, no one ever returned, and that is why the yard is filled with long grasses and weeds. Now the only animals on the farm and in the barn are several flocks of pigeons who reside in the loft and the silo, and our large family of Barn Mice."

"Is it safe to live here?" asked Giuseppe.

"Many things have been destroyed, but we're content here. There is grain, oats and barley in some of the buildings out back, and if we want, we are able to gnaw on old leather harness and horse collars. The garden has some vegetables that grew on their own, like carrots and potatoes, so we are able to survive quite comfortably. You are welcome to stay with us if you wish, but . . . if you wish to return, we'll understand."

"Where are your friends and family?" asked one of the rodents.

Giuseppe told all of them what had happened to his friends and why none of them had returned to the farm. It was an emotional time for Giuseppe, who paused many times to cry.

The Barn Mice assured him that he could stay with them, and their genuine smiles and friendly gestures made it hard for him not to accept.

"I need to think about all of this," said Giuseppe as he paced across the floor of the barn. "All is lost, and I feel alone," he said as he allowed tears to wash his cheeks. He tried to hide his disappointment, but inside his heart was breaking.

Giuseppe spent several days in the cellar of the burned out farmhouse looking for food and several friends, such as Joey and Fritz, but soon realized that life in the farmhouse cellar was far worse than in the barn or in the junk pile with the box spring and mattress. There was nothing in the burned out cellar, and he was now in a quandary.

Several weeks passed, and soon the days grew shorter and the evenings became cooler, warning everyone that fall had arrived. No longer did the Meadowlarks and Red-Winged Blackbirds challenge each other for nesting sites, and the ducks eventually gathered and flew south, leaving the once pristine farm to age.

The threatening autumn weather caused Giuseppe to stay with the Barn Mice. He thought often of his brave friends who had willingly faced life as it came to them. At times he envied their inner strength and resolve to graciously accept their lot in life.

When the snow fell, everyone knew it would be a very difficult winter. Hiding in the barn was a privilege, because there was much food; however, the cold was the worst anyone remembered. Everyone slept in the nursery to keep the infants warm. Their fur grew to be very thick, and many of the old mice perished. Returning to the junk pile was not an option, so Giuseppe accepted the invitation to stay with the Barn Mice.

****

The weather ravaged the mattress and box spring. Bolo and his fellow citizens were fortunate to have escaped when they decided to accept the invitation of the field mice to move to the haystack. It was far more pleasant to live there, so over time they embraced their new home.

Chapter 16

HEARTBREAK

Spring eventually came, and every day Giuseppe spent hours walking about the farmyard and remembering the days, the animals and the activities that had once existed in this place. There were times when he cried at the loss of his friends and the wonderful things they used to do. But when he happened to stop at the hole in the foundation where Frank had run head first into a hole that was too small for him and the prize he carried, he lay on the ground and laughed until he felt dizzy.

On his way back to the barn, he stopped next to a large puddle of water, gazed into it and tried to smile at his reflection. He stared at an old grey-haired rodent, and it was then that he realized that he was old. His whiskers were grey, and his eyelids sagged. The more he studied the reflection, the more he realized that his thoughts and dreams were in his youthful mind but his energy and ability had waned within his weakening limbs. He thought of his family, Angelo and Patrizio, the house fire, the hawks that had snatched his friends and the snake and coyote, but what hurt him more than anything was the thought of his diminishing and ebbing future. Had he wasted his life on impulsive dreams, deteriorating friendships and lack of planning? It was the first time he had thought of his own death. Had he been too impulsive? Was it too late to change? Had he lived with reckless abandon? Did his life have purpose, or was he on a slippery branch over a fast flowing stream? What made him think he would live forever?

Despondent, Giuseppe spent the afternoon and night next to a large downed tree. Downcast, he slept little that night because the faces of all his friends seemed to pass before him. He began to question his ability to survive.

Tears welled up in his eyes as he trudged back to the barn. Near one of the granaries, Giuseppe met a light brown nervous animal that sat up on its hind legs and chirped a whistle sound. Soon other light brown animals scurried out from under the granaries and nervously chirped at him.

Just then a long-legged light tan animal that looked like a coyote approached, and all the chirping animals disappeared under the granaries. Giuseppe was so frightened that he followed one of them to escape. Once they were safe under the granary, one of the chirping animals with large incisor teeth turned to him and asked with a whistle sound, "Who are you?"

"I'm Giuseppe who used to live in the house that burned down. Who are you?"

"My name is Gaston, and I am a prairie dog. Most people call us gophers. Farmers often shoot us, poison us and do what they can to chase us away, but we have nowhere else to go." His eyes narrowed slightly when he had finished speaking.

"Who is that tan-colored animal that is sniffing around as if it wants to catch one of you?" asked Giuseppe.

"He's a coyote, and he would love to eat us, so we are always chirping and warning others of the danger. Hawks swoop down and carry off others, so we have to be very careful."

Gaston introduced Giuseppe to many of the gophers and made him welcome, so he stayed with them for several days and nights.

****

Several days later, Giuseppe exited the barn and made his way to the ruins of the old house. Glass was spread over the ground, along with burned pieces of wood, so he cautiously neared the basement window he had once entered. There was a great mess of flame-marked wood, burned chairs and a couch, as well as a new mattress that had been destroyed. Beside all of this destroyed furniture were broken furnace pipes and several pieces of clothing. Hanging from the floor beam were several summer sausages and a dozen cobs of corn that had been hung there to dry years earlier.

Rain dripped down onto the items in the basement and on Giuseppe. It was too much for him to bear. He tried to wipe the tears from his eyes and was not sure if the water was from the rain or tears.

When his fur was totally soaked, he felt chilled, so he made his way across the farmyard to the barn. When he arrived, he vowed that he would never again leave the safety of the barn. "I will never again go outside or look at that house again."

Hours later, he awakened and found himself on the floor as a wounded beast. His respiration was shallow and irregular, and though he tried to move, his limbs were too stiff and sore, so he closed his eyes and whispered. "This is now my home. I must have outlived all dreams and promises in my life. How did my life pass so quickly?" Sleep overtook him.

****

The cold wind created melancholy moments for Giuseppe, especially when he heard crunchy colored leaves tumbling carelessly across the farmyard. The tenacious breeze carried leaves along roadways and ditches and into open fields. It was a sound of sadness and a warning to all who heard it. Deciduous trees reluctantly surrendered their summer pride to vile gusts of wind that acted so unkindly. Overhead, thick dark white clouds tumbled and rolled, signaling impending changes. Off to the west, the sound of Canada Geese encouraged their flight leader to fly as far and as fast as he could.

Chapter 17

SNOW IMPS

Eventually Herb's headstone was partially buried by cold drifting snow in the Anglican cemetery just outside Thistle, but he knew no discomfort, for he rested comfortably in the arms of his Creator.

Meanwhile, snow imps spun across the sidewalks and roadways in Thistle. Sophie leaned back in her padded chair near the window of Country Lanes Retirement Home to reminisce about former times with a kind Care Giver who brought tea to her room.

As the sun's rays warmed Sophie's cheeks, she closed her eyes and listened to a Bulova mantel clock play twelve melodious notes before striking two o'clock. It, too, had been purchased with Sophie's Visa card, when she had heard the melody at the Hudson's Bay store in the city of Regina.

She smiled as her arthritic hands drew her orange shawl closer to her shoulders and then her cheeks. The colorful yarn had been purchased with her Visa card that now lay in the bottom of the top drawer of her dresser.

Several hours later, she awakened and glanced over to her dresser to look at her two favorite color photos: Herb with the blue suit and orange bowtie she had purchased with her Visa card and a color photo of what she considered to be her son—Oatmeal, her playful Old English Sheepdog.

It seemed inevitable that her eyes were unable to focus upon the snow outside. The tears from her brown eyes never intended to wash away any memories of her two closest friends, but, as Sophie often said, "If your eyes leak, your head will never swell."

~ The End ~

 Jerry Raaf lives in Abbotsford, BC. Several of his books are found in various libraries in western Canada. He has written in a variety of different genres, including a mini-biography entitled *Forever Eleven* and a series of historical novels. Volume I is entitled *Conspiracy with Malicious Intent*, and Volume II is entitled *Eight Days Too Late*. *Conspiracy with Malicious Intent* was awarded a Certificate of Achievement through the Christian Choice Book Awards.

www.ingramcontent.com/pod-product-compliance
Lightning Source LLC
Chambersburg PA
CBHW071005120726
47910CB00004B/1389